DISCOVER YOUR BRAIN

Marie Filch

CONTENTS

1. PART ONE   1

2. I   2

3. 2. B S   7

4. 3. S A   11

5. C   12

6. 4. M E   14

7. H   15

8. 5. R B   18

9. T   19

10. 6. C B   21

11. D   22

12. 7. H P B   24

13. C   25

14. 8. G E   28

15. R   29

16. 9. T S C F   32

17. I   33

18. 10. A V   38

19. T   39

20. 11. T V F   42

21. I   43

22. 12. T R M   47

23. T   48

24. 13. R M   50

25. I   51

26. 14. E D   54

27. B   55

28. 15. R P   57

29. I   58

30. 16. I O   61

31. W   62

32. 17. E R   65

33. I   66

34. 18. S   69

35.	I	70
36.	R R P O	76
37.	PART TWO	77
38.	How Our Brain Changes	78
39.	19. N	79
40.	20. T R C E	84
41.	N	85
42.	21. C R	87
43.	T	88
44.	22. N	93
45.	S	94
46.	23. T C	99
47.	S	100
48.	24. D N	103
49.	L	104
50.	25. E	108
51.	W	109

PART ONE

How Our Brain Fools Us

"Everything we hear is an opinion, not a fact.

Everything we see is a perspective, not the truth."

—Marcus Aurelius

1. P W N E

Scientists have found a module in the left hemisphere of the brain that drives humans to search for a pattern or causal relationship, even when there is no such thing.[2]

I

Neuroplasticity *is a big word driving big excitement. It refers to the brain's ability to change its own structure in ways before thought impossible.*

Atrue-life example will help.

For a few dark moments, imagine your three-year-old granddaughter was in a tragic accident. You're told by physicians that your granddaughter—we'll call her Lorie—has sustained severe brain damage and they're even recommending transferring her to a facility where she can pass in peace.

The damage is extensive. Many of the connections between the two hemispheres of Lorie's brain were either severed or severely damaged. But you notice something the doctors do not. When you look into her eyes, she seems to smile.

This really happened. Grandparents Cal and Janet (names changed) faced this frightful dilemma.

They did not give up. The smiles were the way they communicated with Lorie for months.

Janet wheeled Lorie down the hospital hall and Cal played games with her by hiding behind doors and jumping out yelling, "Boo!"—to which Lorie smiled. Yet the doctors still insisted nothing was there.

Fast forward eight years.

I first met Lorie when her grandfather brought her to a birthday party. She was beaming, chatty, articulate, and exuding an energy level only possible for an eleven-year-old. In every way, she seemed a normal energetic preadolescent, but more mature, as with the ease with which she chatted with her elders. Lorie brought an aura of sunshine and pleasantness to the room that everyone enjoyed. Her grandfather, Cal, was clearly proud of her.

Cal and Janet had not given up. Through the years they dedicated countless hours and persevered with various therapies and learning exercises based on concepts in succeeding chapters.

To prepare for writing this book, I met with Lorie's grandfather for an update. At this writing Lorie is a sophomore in high school and an athlete. She has swimming trophies and is competing with success at state levels. To look at her you would think *Olympian*. She has a ready wit, ribs her grandfather incessantly, and exudes excitement and sunshine.

Lorie's doctors at a prestigious hospital admit they have never been so happy to have been so wrong. She visits them annually, and tests show Lorie has grown many new connections between the two halves of her brain.

Per grandfather Cal, one of Lorie's favorite pastimes is riding in the family convertible (hoping soon to drive it) and playing Neil Diamond with the sound way up to "teenager" level.

One of her favorite songs is Neal Diamond's "Hell Yeah." If Lorie's story fascinates you, envision her riding off in the convertible singing at the top of her lungs with fist pumps in the air. Then look up the song lyrics. You'll gain a new appreciation for the song.

Growing new brain cells is not entirely unexpected of a young child. But at three years old, Lorie's brain was about 80 percent the size it would be as an adult. Could the final growth—20 percent—of Lorie's brain "fit in" to assist?

Lorie's brain was so severely damaged doctors found it difficult to believe. And, back then, scientists believed that current brain cells didn't reproduce.

But Lorie's brain defied all these prior concepts. Lorie's brain pulled off the miracle that is the stuff of neuroplasticity.

So how could her doctors have been so wrong?

Until the end of the twentieth-century, prevailing theories held that, though young children generated new brain cells, the adult human brain was hardwired after early formative years. In other words, upon reaching adulthood, we would develop all the brain cells we would get, and those cells were genetically coded to do certain tasks.

Scientists also knew connections (synapses) between brain cells (neurons) could change and that learning resulted from changing these connections (sprouting dendrites) or strengthening them. The accepted theory of "cells that fire together wire together," drove these concepts. In other words, the neurons that fired together in a chain changed in such a way that made it more likely that firing one would fire the other. Thus, "wired together."

And this was the extent of what scientists thought the brain could do. Now we know differently. Lorie's "neuroplasticity" was well beyond this retail variety of synaptic connection or strengthening. We're talking about wholesale changes previously deemed impossible. The brain is capable of reorganizing itself. The next several chapters discuss these miraculous changes.

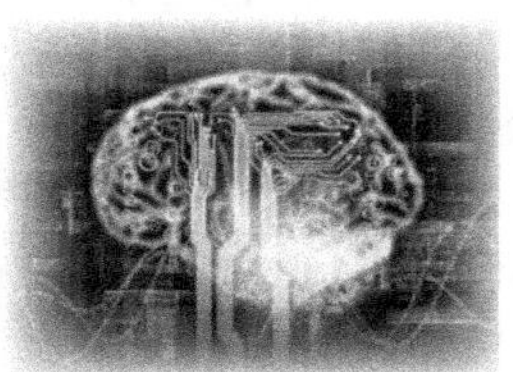

2. BS

*O*ur brain creates filters or shortcuts to avoid tedious processing. That's usually a good thing. But the same process can lead to trouble.

Try reading the following:

I cdnuolt blveiee taht I cluod aulacity uesdnatnrd waht I was rdanieg. Tnahks to the phaonmneal pweor of the hmuan mnid, aoccdrnig to rscheearchres at Cmabrigde Uinervtisy, it dseno't mtaetr in what oerdr the ltteres in a wrod are, the olny iproamtnt tihng is taht the frsit and lsat ltteer be in the rghit pclae.

Despite the words above being absurdly misspelled, chances are you were able to understand the whole thing. That's because over your years of reading, your brain has developed shortcuts to spare itself from processing every single letter of a word.

In this case, that's a blessing, because it makes your reading quicker and easier.

But mental shortcuts also have their disadvantages as well. To experience one for yourself, watch a short video about selective attention at Youtube.com. Search for "Selective Attention Test from Simon and Chabris (1999)"; when you're done, continue reading.

Did you spot the gorilla brazenly walking across the room—and even pausing to beat his chest—as the players passed around the basketball?

If you didn't, you're not alone. About 50 percent of viewers are so focused on counting passes that they entirely miss the ape.

And if something that big and hairy can be overlooked, it's worth considering how many other times our reliance on mental shortcuts to breeze through our daily routines is blinding us to the extraordinary.

Want to test yourself again? Try watching the spin-off video. Go to Youtube.com and search "Selective Attention Test 2.0"; when you are done, continue reading.

Almost everyone spots the gorilla tackling the banana.

But almost no one notices the dancing chicken.

That's in part because the latter video has more going on than the previous one, but it's also because it plays on your brain's tendency to create shortcuts that focus on the familiar and expected. The previous video trained you to look out for a gorilla, so this time you spotted the banana while it acted like an ape by beating its chest, and then the actual gorilla, but at the expense of seeing something that was entirely new.

Let's apply this principal to something more familiar than gorillas or chickens. Have you ever looked for the jar of mayonnaise in the refrigerator and couldn't find it? Then you called your spouse, parent, or roommate over only to have them spot it right in front of your nose?

Chances are your brain's filtering mechanisms were active because the scene before you was all too familiar.

Here's how to find the mayonnaise. Try a different perspective. Take a step

to the side, kneel, or maybe step up on a stool. You will have a less familiar perspective and your brain will do less filtering. This applies not just to finding the mayo, but any difficulty with visual input. For example, if you are having trouble understanding an email, print it out and read it on paper instead of on the screen.[13]

In summary, we wouldn't be nearly as efficient without our mental shortcuts. Paying attention to every little thing all the time wouldn't merely be exhausting, but it would so bombard us with extraneous information that we'd end up paralyzed from information overload.

Nonetheless, many of us filter too much of our lives through short-cuts and past expectations instead of seeing the world clearly. So we should try to go into any situation with both our minds and eyes wide open, seeking different perspectives, so we can experience what's truly happening in the moment— and so we can fully appreciate sudden encounters with the new and amazing.

3. S A

O*ur minds have an autopilot much more suited for some tasks than our conscious mind.*

lose your eyes and imagine driving down the road and making a lane change, one lane to the right. Take your time and go through the actual motions.

Easily done, right?

C

If you are like most people you held the wheel straight, then turned it slightly right for a moment, and then straightened it back out. Simple.

The problem is, if you did the exercise the way most people do, you piloted a course right off the road onto the sidewalk!

The correct motion is banking slightly right and then back *through the center* to the left, the same distance you went right, and then finally straightening out.[14] If you don't believe it, go for a drive and test it.

Disconnects between our subconscious mind and our conscious, reasoning mind can be beneficial (such as driving a car without thinking through every move or riding a bicycle or just plain walking). In fact, in sports, athletes undergo significant mental training to let go of conscious step-by-step thoughts. Likewise, musicians couldn't play melodically if they consciously thought about which key to press or which string to fret. They learn to quit thinking and let their subconscious minds take over.

This is wonderful for music or athletics or just everyday living. And, as we discussed in the last chapter, our minds would be overloaded if we had to think consciously about every action.

But this autonomy can also be a problem. Our subconscious minds can drive thoughts leading to poor decisions. The next couple of chapters will explore a few of those influences and suggest ways to overcome them.

4. ME

Simple exposure to a concept, object, or person can have a pronounced effect on our opinions, well beyond our conscious thought processing. ave you ever bought an item only because you were familiar with the brand? Or voted for a candidate only because you were more familiar with the name?

We all have. But just how impressionable are we, and how easily can we be manipulated?

H

Renowned social psychologist Robert Zajonc wanted to find out. He first contrived a series of nonsense words like *kadirga* or *diliki* and then asked American listeners to guess whether each word meant something good or bad in Turkish. Results: the more often a word was repeated, the more likely the listener guessed a positive meaning.

Then Zajonc tried a similar experiment, this time visual. He projected twenty irregular octagonal shapes onto a dimly lit screen for only a single millisecond, fast enough so viewers could not make out the shape, or any image at all. Then he showed a second series of images with two shapes, a new one, and one from the previous deck. This time each slide was visible for a full second. He then asked which one the viewer liked better. Participants overwhelmingly chose from the first series—even though it was almost indistinguishable to the naked eye.

Why?

Consider evolution. Our brains had to evolve to pay most attention to something novel—good or bad. If we had exposure to something over and over and it didn't bite or hurt us, we became more comfortable with it. And with comfort came a more positive attitude toward it.

Zajonc called this the "mere-exposure effect,"[15] and it's an example of how our likes, dislikes, and choices are not totally conscious. They are often influenced by our hardwired, biased brain in combination with experiences.

Advertisers know this, so we hear brand names over and over. Likewise, publicity, even bad, is a major advantage in politics. Consider the 2016 presidential election. Then-candidate Donald Trump expended great effort to make the news every day. Even though it was not always good news, it kept his name in front of people. It worked.

So, at decision time, we need to take a step back and carefully think through our reasons and consider whether mere exposure is unduly influencing our thought process. The off-brand jeans may be just as good as the Levi's. Or maybe the candidate with the familiar name isn't the most qualified. We need to be aware of all this "noise" in our exposures and take a step back and think with the reasoning part of our minds.

5. RB

Though it's common knowledge we better remember the most recent things, we seldom realize how this tendency cripples our decisions.

T

He concept of recency bias is related to the pattern problems and mere exposure issues we discussed above. We instinctively know about recency. It's easiest to recall the last number on a list or the last

thing our colleague said. Psychologists have proven this myriad times. That's why salespeople ask to be the last presenter.

But this recency tendency spills over into our decision-making process in a way that may not be beneficial.

We are more likely to estimate probabilities on a "handful of the *latest* outcomes," as opposed to more appropriate long-term data.[16] Jason Zweig, author of *Your Money and Your Brain*, tells us, "A survey of forecasts by hundreds of individual investors found their expectations of stock returns over the next six months were more than twice as dependent on what the stock market did last week than what it did over the previous few months."[17] Additionally, we assign the *probability* of an outcome by the ease with which we can call it to mind—and the more recent, the easier it is to recall.[18]

Pair recency and ease of recollection with our pattern recognition faults, and we see why investors fall into reasoning traps. From pattern recognition, we think if a stock has gone up each of the last two or three days, it will probably keep going up.

And the recency bias makes us focus on the most recent, and not the best horizon for analysis. Much better data exists. For example, Fidelity Investments recommends analyzing security performance over various horizons such as tactical (one to twelve months), business cycle (one to ten years), and secular (ten to thirty years).

In summary, it's difficult to escape these faulty influences and it may take significantly more work to overcome them. But the effort should yield much better results over the long term. When it comes to investments or other decisions, business or personal, we must remember the recent trend is no substitute for careful analyses—statistical or other.

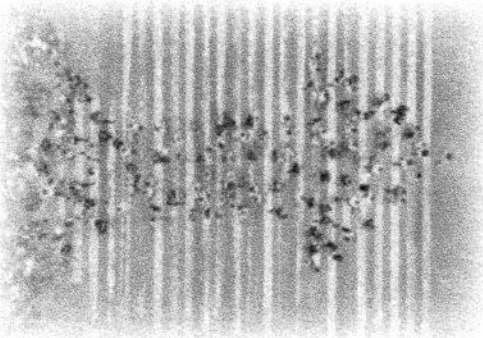

6. CB

We naturally want to be right. And we'll go to great lengths to prove we are, sometimes at the expense of truth.

D

O you ever search for information to prove yourself wrong?

Likely not often.

We all want to be right, so we seek information to confirm our opinions. We search for support rather than seeking information that could contradict us.

This is especially relevant in the political arena. Conservatives are more likely to watch Fox News, while liberals are more likely to watch MSNBC. Before cable TV, news broadcasters took pride in an unbiased delivery of news. But in an age of instant information, and *lots* of it, many media outlets have evolved (or devolved) to presenting an unabashed slant on the news.

Now that we have choices, we seek the channels that agree with us.

But is this really in our best interest?

For our own growth and those around us we need to check out both sides. And we can try getting news from a more neutral source. It's critical for the education of our electorate, the maintenance of a healthy democracy, and our own personal welfare.

It isn't just politics. You may have an opinion on the best way to ______________ (insert any topic you want in here), and you'll most likely find someone to confirm it. Just remember, in Columbus's time it was easy to find people to "confirm" the world was flat.

The herd instinct is a product of the confirmation bias. We seek our confirmation in the common behavior of others.

Advertisers use this extensively as they convince us "everyone is doing it," commonly known as the "bandwagon" approach. We all recognize it. Who's mom didn't say, "Just because everyone else is jumping over the cliff doesn't mean you should, too!" But it's hard to escape. To join the crowd is part of our genetic make-up.

The solution is to be aware. Since we are all human beings, we will most likely have the same bias as the crowd, positive or negative. Your mom was right when she told you, "Think for yourself." Beware the herd.

7. H P B

Not only do we want to be right, we want to be precisely right at the risk of becoming wrong. And we tend to remember getting things right even when we didn't.

C

An you think of a time when you correctly predicted an outcome? Did you think, "I just knew it?" Or, "Nailed it?"

Maybe you did . . . or . . . maybe not. Scientists have identified a quirk called hindsight bias. It's a tendency to look back on your prior thoughts or predictions and think you correctly forecasted an event or outcome.

A study was done in 1972 when President Richard Nixon went to China, the first visit by a U.S. president since China turned communist. No one knew what would happen, and the trip was thought a considerable risk. But the trip yielded significant successes for both countries with a pledge to normalize relations.

Just before the trip, dozens of Israeli university students were asked to predict the probability of success. Afterwards, the students were queried about the accuracy of their predictions. Less than two weeks after the trip, 71 percent remembered foretelling a higher probability of success than their documented prediction. Four months after the trip, 81 percent claimed a higher accuracy rate than their actual prediction.[19]

So before we proclaim our visionary prowess, we need to consider the hindsight bias. If we really want to know if we or others are clairvoyant, jotting down the forecast is the only sure proof.

This imperative to be right comes with another quirk. We also aspire to be *precisely* right.

Franck Schuurman, consultant for Decision Strategies International, runs a simple exercise in his lectures. He asks questions like, "In what year was Mozart born?," with a challenge to have 90 percent confidence the correct answer will fall in a chosen range. Respondents could narrowly guess 1730 to 1770, or more broadly, 1600 to 1900. Interestingly, the majority get only five of ten questions correct because they use too a narrow range.[20] They could easily pick a broader range with much higher probability of success. But they insist on precision—or being "more correct."

Unnecessary precision can affect decisions and make you wrong more than you wish. There's nothing wrong with going for a tolerable range if it suits the purpose.

Perhaps that's why your cable TV company tells you their tech will be there sometime between 8:00 a.m. and 5:00 p.m.? Maybe they forgot the "tolerable" part.

8. GE

Our expectations can be influenced by things totally unrelated to the object of assessment.

R

Ead the following description of a person called Jim:

Jim is intelligent, skillful, industrious, warm, determined, practical, and cautious. Mark the one trait in each pair that most likely represents Jim:

Generous-------Not Generous

Unhappy--------Happy

Irritable----------Good-natured

Humorous-------Humorless

Seventy-five to 95 percent of people think Jim is generous, happy, good natured, and humorous. However, when the word *warm* is changed to *cold*, only 5 to 35 percent think Jim will have these traits.[21]

We think if a person has good qualities in one area, he or she will have good qualities in other areas. Scientists call this the "the halo effect."

Human resource managers will admit that better-looking people have an edge in getting hired. Likewise, people who perform well in their operative job are often thought better prospects for management, despite not necessarily displaying management skills.

These positive associations extend beyond observable characteristics to other sensory experiences.

Experiment participants were handed either a warm cup of coffee or a cold drink from a complete stranger. Those receiving the warm coffee were more likely to consider the stranger to be a "warm person."[22]

Our subconscious expectations influence us even though we know they should not.

However, these expectations can be used to our benefit.

A study analyzed patients recovering from abdominal surgery. One group was told what to expect, such as how long the pain would last, what type of pain they would experience, and when they would regain consciousness. The other group was told nothing. Patients who were told what to expect experienced less pain, required less medication, and recovered earlier than those who were told nothing.

In summary, expectations are a powerful influence, driven not only by hardwired subconscious predispositions like the "halo effect" but also by our conscious expectations. We need to be aware of this influence and carefully reason through our perceptions. But the good news is expectations can also be used in a positive manner as we'll discuss further in several chapters in Part Two.

9. TSCF

*O*ur minds can easily deceive us when it comes to matters of relative costs and benefits.

I

Magine you arrived at your local movie theater, reached into your pocket for the twenty-dollar general admission ticket you purchased an hour ago, and discovered that you'd lost it. Would you buy another ticket?

Alternatively, imagine that you didn't purchase anything in advance, but when arriving at the theater, you reached into your pocket and realized that you'd lost the twenty-dollar bill you were planning to use for admission. Would you still buy the ticket?

Princeton University psychologists Daniel Kahneman and Amos Tversky ran these two scenarios by test subjects back in 1984 (albeit with cheaper tickets; I've adjusted for inflation).

As it turned out, 88 percent of those who imagined losing the twenty-dollar bill said they'd go ahead and buy the ticket.

But only 46 percent of those who imagined losing the ticket said they'd buy a replacement ticket.[23] Why the difference?

Financially, the same thing happened across the board—everyone lost twenty dollars.

But those who imagined losing the twenty-dollar bill didn't attach that loss to the ticket. They therefore had little reason to not simply fish out another twenty dollars and see the movie as planned. In other words, they mentally wrote off the loss, forgot about it, and moved on with their lives.

In contrast, the second group was dealing with the pain of not only losing money, but of taking the risk of exchanging something they possessed—the twenty-dollar bill—for something they didn't—the movie ticket—and having it turn out badly. On an emotional level they probably weren't even aware of, they didn't want to immediately take a similar risk that might make them feel even worse (e.g., "What if I paid another twenty dollars, for a total of forty dollars, and it turned out the movie sucked?").

At the same time, not buying another ticket mitigated the pain by letting them tell themselves they hadn't lost anything beyond what they'd already planned—because they'd intended to spend twenty dollars, and that's what ended up happening.

However, all of that is irrational. The truth is the first and second tickets actually have nothing to do with each other. Seeing the movie was worth twenty dollars when the first ticket was purchased, and the movie hadn't changed an hour later, so it continued to be worth twenty dollars; and that's the only factor worth considering if looked at unemotionally.

While the stakes were relatively low in this scenario—not seeing a movie —the tendency to care more about what we've lost, or what we're at risk of losing, than what we can gain is actually hardwired into our brains. In the past, it had genuine value for our survival. But in our modern era dominated by continual change, this way of thinking—sometimes referred to as the "sunk cost fallacy"—can be a major handicap.

For example, those who play the stock market should base their decisions to sell or buy based solely on the most current and accurate information available to them. However, many people keep in mind what they paid for a stock, and will hold onto even a clear loser as it keeps falling lower and lower in the hope that it somehow goes back up again to at least the price they originally paid—because they want to avoid the emotional pain of admitting to a choice that turned out badly and of feeling, even for a moment, like a failure.

Investors have lost millions of dollars this way.

There are also many instances of the sunk cost fallacy in business. For example, Kodak dominated the photography market from the 1900s through the 1970s, but it made most of its profits from selling film, and its leaders wouldn't emotionally accept the industry's switch to film-less digital photography—even though one of its own employees invented the first digital camera in 1975! Had Kodak adapted to the times, it could've become a major player in smart phone cameras, or another Facebook or Instagram. But by refusing to let go of its past investments in film, Kodak grew disconnected from its customers, and the company has now all but disappeared.

You may be able to think of sunk cost fallacy experiences in your own life —for example, dating someone who wasn't really the right fit, or hanging onto a stressful job, for a lot longer than was good for you.

If so, you were only being human.

The old saying "A bird in the hand is worth two in the bush" reflects this mentality. While it might at first sound like common sense, the sunk cost fallacy is telling you to value what you already possess over what you have the potential to achieve.

Instead, you should take a close look at what you're holding onto, and consider whether you might be better off letting it go—to free your hands to receive something of far greater value.

10. A V

When our mind is assigning value it can be tricked rather easily.

T

He sunk cost fallacy is one quirk in how we perceive value. Are there others?

Imagine you are in morning rush hour at the main subway station in Washington, D.C. An ordinary man dressed in jeans and a baseball cap takes out his violin and performs with extraordinary ability. He plays some of the most difficult pieces ever written for violin. What would you think? An incredibly talented street performer?

In 2007 the *Washington Post* sponsored an undercover field story that created the scenario above. During the forty-three-minute concert, there was no thunderous applause and no cameras flashing. In fact, of the 1,097 people who walked by, hardly anyone stopped to listen.

No one knew at the time, but the man in the baseball cap was Joshua Bell, one of the finest violinists alive, a regular performer to *sold-out* crowds in the most prestigious concert halls. And his violin was a $3,500,000 Stradivarius. But since he wasn't dressed in formal attire, and there was no stage, Mr. Bell looked like an ordinary street performer and passersby saw and heard only an ordinary street musician.[24]

To be fair, many distractions played into the subway experiment. Commuters were rushing to work, and the acoustics and noisiness of the environment weren't conducive to a good concert experience.

But what if an experiment were designed with just one variable: price?

Dan Ariely, a professor of psychology and behavior economics at Duke University, set up such an experiment using SoBe Adrenaline Rush, a beverage claiming to increase mental acuity. He developed a thirty-minute word jumble to assess the effects of the drink related to price and administered it to three different groups of students.

One group was told about the intelligence-enhancing properties and asked to watch a video while allowing time for the drink to take effect. They were also required to sign an authorization allowing researchers to charge their university account $2.89.

A second group was given the drink, the story, and video, but were told the university got a discount, and were only charged eighty-nine cents for the drink.

A third group, the control group, took the test without drinking SoBe or watching the video.

The results were interesting. The group charged $2.89 for the drink did, in fact, do slightly better than the control group. But the group who drank the "cheaper" SoBe performed *significantly worse* than the control group!

Ariely's summation was this: "The intriguing idea is that expectations change the reality we live in. When you get something at a discount, the

positive expectations don't kick in as strongly."

But what if it's free? Are expectations the same? Next chapter.

11. TV F

*O*ur minds confuse "free" and real value.

I

In an earlier chapter we found we're hardwired to avoid loss, and so value what we have over what we can potentially gain. In the last chapter, we learned our expectations can also cause errant value

judgments.

An interesting off-shoot of these phenomena is our love affair with things that are free.

In his bestselling book *Predictably Irrational,* Dan Ariely relates an experiment he conducted with chocolate. Ariely set up a table in a large public building to sell two items: a Hershey's Kiss for a penny or a Lindt truffle for fifteen cents. (Dated prices based on the time of the experiment.) Customers were allowed to buy only one piece of chocolate, so they had to choose between the two offerings.

A Hershey's Kiss normally costs around six cents, so one cent was an excellent price.

And a Lindt truffle, which is a significantly higher quality of chocolate, normally costs around thirty-five cents, so fifteen cents was an even better price.

The clear bargain was the Lindt truffle, which offered a discount of around twenty cents vs. the Hershey's Kiss being discounted for around five cents; plus, the truffle tasted way better.

And that was borne out by sales. A whopping 73 percent of customers bought the Lindt truffle.

Then Ariely lowered the price of both chocolates by a penny. As a result, the Lindt truffle became fourteen cents, and the Hershey's Kiss became free.

While a one cent change might seem trivial, it made a world of difference. The free Hershey's Kiss won over 69 percent of the customers, a result nearly opposite of the previous one—even though the Lindt truffle remained a greater bargain and tastier choice.

To make sure this wasn't an aberration, Ariely ran several variants of the experience (changing the types of chocolates, eliminating anyone's need to have spare change, etc.). They all ended up with the same result.

Why did the switch to free make such a powerful difference?

Because, as a previous chapter explained, we're wired to be wary of giving up what we have for what we can obtain. And when we make a choice that doesn't end well, we're wired to feel awful about it.

When something is free, though, it bypasses that entire mental mechanism. If we're paying nothing, then we don't have to worry about potential loss, because we're not giving up anything we own or putting anything at risk.

In other words, a free item literally frees us to act without our usual mental baggage.

That's why so many companies offer products for free to get you involved as a customer. They know it's a big hurdle to convince you to buy something you've never tried before, because you're nervous about not liking it and then having to deal with a feeling of loss. But if you try a product for free, you can avoid both financial and emotional risk—and have the chance of deciding you really do like the product and want to make it a part of your life.

That said, Ariely's chocolate experiment also demonstrates the downside of choosing free things. When you choose something that costs you nothing over something that's actually better for you, you're cheating yourself of a superior experience.

For example, if you stay home to watch TV to enjoy something you truly love, such as an amazing drama or comedy series, or the day's news, that's great. But if you're watching TV only because it's free—or because you've already paid for it—then you should consider going out more to experience live events and interact with new people. It'll cost money, but it'll be worth it for the new experiences and relationships you gain.

So "free" is wonderful if it eases us into trying something new that might merit our time and attention. But we should beware of reflexively choosing something free over something that's likely to provide us with a richer, fuller life.

12. T R M

We value real money differently than equivalent cash substitutes such as credit cards or cash replacements, sometimes leading us into irresponsible actions.

o demonstrate this, Dan Ariely (as noted before) conducted studies with MIT and Harvard students in which participants were told to solve as many math problems as they could in five minutes. One group was told to submit their sheets and they would get paid 50 cents for each correct answer. A second group was told to tear up their answer sheets and simply tell the experimenter their score in exchange for payment, making it possible to cheat. The third was told was told the same as the second, except rather than cash, they would receive a token for each right answer that they could then exchange for cash just twelve feet across the room

G uess what? The participants who received tokens lied much more than those who were paid directly in physical cash. The honest group solved an average of 3.5 correctly. The tear-up-the-sheet-and-get-cash-group reported 6.2 correct questions. But the "tear up sheet and get tokens" group proffered a whopping 9.4 questions "solved."

In other words, those working with cash substitutes were much more willing to indulge in self-deceit and rationalization.[25] Ariely says it's much easier to be dishonest when we are one step removed from cash. And that includes deceiving ourselves.

The ramifications of this experiment become apparent when considering credit cards. We're likely to spend more quickly, in larger amounts, and with less pain when paying with plastic than with cash. (In fact, numerous subsequent studies have confirmed this.)

So if you find yourself perpetually running low on funds, consider paying more often with hard cash.

Alternatively, if you're buying online, try picturing yourself paying the amount with a one-, five-, ten-, or twenty-dollar bill before you click to approve the purchase.

Another helpful practice is to pay each credit card bill as soon as it comes in. This trains your mind to recognize that those intangible numbers end up translating at the end of the month into real money.

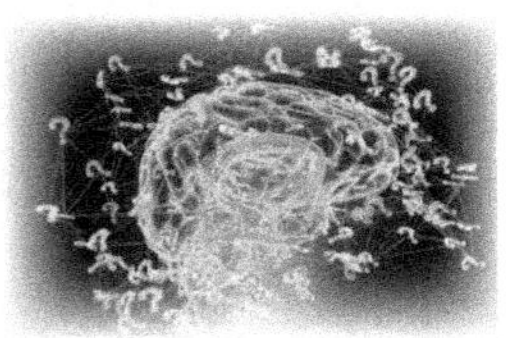

13. R M

Memories are reconstructed every time we recall them. In the process we tend to distort them, sometimes to a great extent, even recalling false memories.

I

T turns out our personal memories aren't nearly as reliable as we think. It doesn't mean memories are useless, but we need to understand a few alarming principles, principles that affect our actions and decisions.

In 1992 a cargo plane crashed into an Amsterdam apartment building. Less than a year later, 55 percent of the Dutch population recalled watching TV and seeing the plane hit the building, with many able to recall specifics such as the angle of descent or whether the plane was on fire before crashing.

But there was a problem.

The event was never caught on video! The mass recollection had been pieced together from descriptions and pictures of the event.[26]

Our memories are made from bits and scraps reconstructed whenever a recollection takes place. That means each recollection from the past may trigger the addition of new details, shading of the facts, or even pruning of a few key facts. And we don't realize we're doing so.[27]

It's not difficult to implant a false memory. Psychologist Elizabeth Loftus at the University of Washington conducted an experiment during which she gave volunteers a booklet narrating three true stories from each volunteer's childhood plus an added false story describing being lost in the mall at age five. When asked later to write down all they could remember about the events, 25 percent were sure all four events were real![28]

Other cognitive scientists have provided evidence that false memory is a normal occurrence. One study observed that adult twins often disagree about which one experienced an event in childhood. For example, they might differ in their recollection of which twin, at age eight, was pushed off the bike by the neighbor. Even the most basic information like who was involved can get "rearranged."[29]

For more information on this fascinating topic, search for Elizbeth Loftus as noted above. She's done extensive work on memory issues.

So the next time we argue with our spouse or friend over what happened ten years ago, we may want to consult books, documents, yearbooks, the Web (maybe, as we'll discuss later) or something more reliable than our memory.

Likewise, we shouldn't start thinking we are getting senile when we lose the argument about what happened. We're just being human, again!

14. E D

Our brain will devote little energy to storing information it can easily access externally.

efore we become too critical of our poor overworked brain, we need to give it credit for fuel-efficiency in allocating resources. Scientists believe our brain evolved to use as little energy as possible. Back in the early days, our species didn't know when the next meal was coming. An energy-efficient brain was an evolutionary advantage that remains today despite our ready availability of brain fuel. As noted in pattern discussion, our brains would quickly become overloaded if we processed every detail. So evolution and necessity has taught our brains to work only as hard as necessary. And our brain may do that without us consciously knowing it.

$$B$$

As an example, today we have the Google phenomenon. If we hear or read a fact, and we know we can easily look it up on Google, our brain will expend little or no effort trying to memorize it.[30] We go into power-saving mode. All we remember is what is required to find the fact again. In this case, a few touches or clicks of the mouse.

We can avoid this quirk by giving cues to our brain to switch on memory. As an example, we could envision needing to know first aid or the location of a hospital during a medical emergency, where no phone signal is available.

Gord Hotchkiss, past chairman of the Search Marketing Professionals Association (and an expert in online user behavior), thinks this same powersaving principle is at work in communications.

According to Hotchkiss, "Face-to-face communication can put a huge cognitive load on our brains. We're receiving communication on a much greater bandwidth than with text. When we're across from a person, we not only hear what they're saying, we're reading emotional cues, watching facial expression, interpreting body language, and monitoring vocal tones."[31] So it's no surprise that texting is becoming the communication mode of choice for many people. It's less cognitive load.

As we all know, the course of least resistance is not always the best. At the extreme level it's not good practice to propose to the future bride by text. Likewise, that conversation with the boss about performance and a potential raise, warrants all the cognitive resources we can muster. We can all think of many more examples along the continuum.

So maybe there is a good reason for that next meeting we were dreading to attend?

15. R P

We tend to over-rely on the past as an indicator of the future, even when we know conditions in the future are different.

I

Magine you are in the class of Professor J. Keith Murnighan of Northwestern University. He's running an exercise for his MBA students where he auctions off a real twenty-dollar bill with simple, but

strongly stated, rules.[32]

1. Bidding proceeds in dollar increments and the highest bidder gets the twenty-dollar bill.

2. The second highest bidder also pays what he or she bid and *gets nothing.*

3. It *is* for real money.

So are you willing to pay a dollar or two or all the way up to nineteen dollars for a twenty?

Murnighan notes it's easy to get the bidding going. Many students set limits for themselves as they have in prior auctions. But, the rules in this auction soon make that thinking irrelevant. Not surprisingly, after the bidding reaches twenty dollars, most everyone drops out except the last two bidders. If you find yourself in second place, you'll pay anyway, so why not bid another two dollars to avoid paying nineteen dollars for nothing? The problem is deciding when to stop and accept that other bidders will think the same and send you on an endless journey like mice on a wheel.

It's not unusual for the "winner" to pay fifty dollars for the auctioned twenty-dollar bill and the loser to pay forty-nine dollars for nothing. In one case, the loser paid in excess of one hundred dollars! Remember, according to the rules, the loser pays his last bid too. So there is motivation to keep bidding to win twenty dollars to partially offset your losses.

The emotional components of this exercise clouded decision-making, as we'll discuss later. But the students' historical familiarity with the auction process misled them into major pitfalls. Though they heard the rule about second place paying, they weren't deterred. Murnighan often does a second auction right after the first and students fall into the same trap.

Reasoning through pitfalls is not easy when our historical reference point is strong. When emotions take over, and we realize we are in over our head, we will find it difficult to think rationally. Though the students understood the rules, something in their brain latched on to prior auction experience rather than looking forward and analyzing potential consequences.

Business research has determined that companies often make decisions based on past occurrences, without evaluating current trends in customer behavior, market, or environmental conditions.

Almost half of the twenty-five exemplar companies in Tom Peters and Robert Waterman's 1982 book, *In Search of Excellence,* are no longer in business. Likewise, of the original S&P 500 list created in 1957, only 15 percent are still on the list today. Many of these companies failed because they became overconfident that past successful strategies would work again in the future.[33]

So when we make our decisions, it's important to examine our scaffold or framework that evolved from our past experiences, and then consider new information that could, and should, change our understanding.

So how much information do we need? Next chapter.

16.10

Information overload is real. Our brain can only process limited amounts of data.

H en was the last time you checked Google for decision information? Likely recently. Why not? It's the ultimate knowledge base. With Google we get as much information and

as many (emphasis on *"as many"*) comparisons as we choose.

Are we making better decisions? Scientists say maybe not.

In fact, research in decision science shows people faced with too many choices are likely to make no decision at all.

Sheena Ivengar at Columbia University studied participation in business 401(k) programs and found participation declined from 75 to 70 percent when the choices went from 2 to 11. Participation further dropped to just 61 percent when the options went to 59.[34] (If you are unfamiliar with 401(k) programs, the incentive is significant: not enrolling in a 401(k) is like throwing money away. Employers typically match a percentage of employees' contributions.) This is a simple example of information overload. Other studies in more impactful areas, such as air traffic and medicine, reveal the same result. The bottom line is, we can only process so much information.

So how do we deal with information overload?

In earlier chapters we discussed ways to override information from our subconscious brain. But it has a purpose, and this is one of them. Researchers have found creative decisions are more likely to bubble up from a brain applying unconscious thought as opposed to a full-frontal analytical assault."[35] A decision requiring assessment of complex information is not best approached by methodical and conscious means. Results may be better and regrets fewer if we give our subconscious mind time to process the info and remove ourselves from the inflow. The adage, "sleep on it," has merit.

We should set our priorities, too. If the decision hinges on a few criteria, we should concentrate on those and not get bogged down by irrelevant data. Some people naturally do this. Take TV channel surfers. The "deciders" just find an acceptable program and stop. The "maximizers," search endlessly, absorbing all kinds of information and struggling with a decision.[36]

So, are you a decider or a maximizer? We need to learn to be deciders if a decision is required and hinges on a few criteria. Maximizers have their place, though. Sometimes a decision is secondary to seeking new experiences, like searching for a vacation destination or looking for a new book to read.

17. E R

Emotions can have an over-sized impact on our risk assessments.

En a simple experiment, volunteers were told to imagine being called to the doctor's office for an urgent medical matter. Another group was not burdened with imagining such a stressful event. Both groups were then asked to pick between a relatively safe 60 percent chance of winning five dollars or a riskier 30 percent chance of winning ten dollars. The anxietyinduced people were much more likely to take the safe bet.[37] This simple experiment illustrates how we fail to understand that our emotional response from one event can affect our ability to make decisions regarding an unrelated event.

1

The anxiety factor can be even more complex. In another study, men were asked to think of either three or eight factors increasing their chances of heart disease. Those who named only three factors rated their overall risk of heart disease higher than those who were forced to think of eight.

Experimenters concluded that men forced to think of eight had to work much harder. (Try coming up with eight yourself!) They subconsciously thought, *If it's that hard to think of eight reasons, my risk must not be that great!* Conversely, those who had to think of only three found the short list easier to recall, making the risk seem more real.[38] Herein we find a serious problem with assessing risk: *the easier to call to mind, the more real the risk seems.*

This "ease to call to mind" is influenced by other factors.

"Recency," as discussed earlier, is one.

But even more powerful is how vivid the event seems. For example, people pay twice as much for hospitalization insurance for a specific disease than for a policy that covers any medical issue. "Any issue" is vague but "cancer" is vivid.[39]

Likewise, people fear an attack, clear the beach, and even stay away from the ocean altogether at the slightest mention of, "Shark!"

But the odds of being killed in a shark attack are 1 in 3,943,110! Compare that to the odds of dying in a motor vehicle accident: 1 in 88! But we don't think twice about climbing into our cars every day. Thanks to movies like *Jaws* we can envision those ferocious shark teeth. We can easily recall the image and trigger an anxious response, coloring our perception of probability.

Even an alarming word or phrase can factor into our anxiety response.

Elizabeth Loftus conducted an experiment where participants were shown videos of car accidents. Some were asked how fast the cars were going when they "hit each other." Others were asked how fast they were going when they "smashed into each other." Both groups were shown the same videos, but the ones prompted by the words "smashed into" estimated the speed 19 percent faster.[40] "Smashed" is more vivid than "hit." Part of the solution is simply to be aware.

We can mitigate the recency issue by putting time in between an event and our decision. But the vivid images issue is difficult to overcome. Many people are still much more anxious about flying than driving despite flying being safer. We must keep telling ourselves that the statistics are true and try to recruit that reasoning part of our brain.

18. S

We prefer stories as opposed to good data to support our decisions, sometimes resulting in sub-optimal actions.

I

Magine you are considering buying a new car and check *Consumer Reports* to find a highly reliable choice. But then you go to a party and find a friend bought the very same vehicle and complains he takes it to

the repair shop often. He says, "nothing but trouble."

Will you buy that car?

If you're like most people, you won't. The account from your friend will have more bearing on your decision than the statistics. But should it? Your friend is a sample of one, while the *Consumer Reports* data are based on large numbers of vehicles. There is variance in everything, and even the bestmade cars have an occasional "lemon." It could be that your friend got one of these rare lemons, or maybe he or she hasn't kept up with the recommended maintenance.

The point is, by not buying the car you'd be basing your decision on one person's narrative, not reliable statistical data.[41] But excluding the story from your decision is difficult.

Our fondness for stories is hardwired in us. In the history of humankind, only recently have we been able to record and store accessible facts for the knowledge we need. Prior to such capabilities, we passed our history and knowledge from generation to generation by telling stories.

We all love a good story. We have an evolved penchant for paying close attention to them.[42] But, our preference for stories or anecdotal evidence over facts and figures can be a problem. It intertwines with our "ease to call to mind" issue. Stories are much easier to remember than statistics.

This tendency is not lost on politicians. In recent elections "toughening up on crime" was brought up frequently. We hear story after story of violent crimes and get the impression crime is running rampant. Our media feeds us a steady diet of gruesome news. News outlets have the motto "If it bleeds, it leads." Such reporting tricks us into feeling the world is becoming more dangerous. Campaigning politicians capitalize on this fear and run on platforms dedicated to beefing up police forces and cracking down on gang violence. They share the tragic and/or scary stories of crime victims. No one could argue that these incidents are not problematic, and we would all agree we should do more. But we need perspective in decisions on policy.

The truth is violent crime in the U.S. was down by 51 percent between 1993 and 2018, the most recent data available. Likewise, property crime was down 54 percent over the same period.[43] Note the graphs below courtesy of the Pew Research Center, Washington, D.C., October 17, 2019.

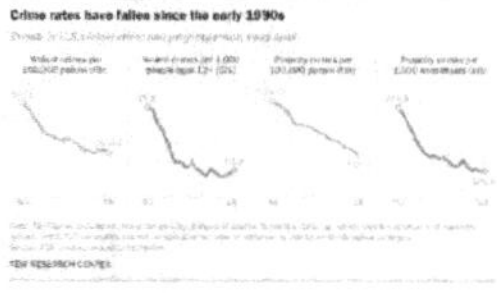

So, despite the nightly news, the country is not "going to hell in a handbasket." But politicians know we believe and relate to stories. They will rely on anecdotal evidence to raise anxiety levels and garner votes.

We can't blame politicians for using stories. It is effective. But we all must realize the stories we're hearing in the news give us a false impression. Case in point, the subject of school shootings has significantly raised anxiety for both parents and students. Rightly so, given the headlines. But according to author James Alan Fox of *The Wiley Handbook on Violence in Education, 2018,* "There is not an epidemic of school shootings."

In his book, Fox notes that there were four times as many children shot and killed in schools in the early 1990s compared with more recent statistics. In fact, more children are killed every year drowning in pools or in bicycle accidents than in school shootings. Fox is quick to point out that this doesn't mean we should ignore the problem, but policy-makers need to base decisions on facts, allowing for a reasoned response that doesn't unnecessarily scare people or infringe on civil liberties.[44] Overly militarizing schools with armed guards or educators may only add to anxiety.

The same concept applies internationally. Our daily diet of journalism would have us believe the world is getting more violent every day. But it isn't, even considering terrorist attacks. According to Nigel Barber, PhD, "The worldwide probability of dying in a terrorist attack is infinitesimal, at less than one in a million per year. The risk is three times lower than in the 1980s. Yet, survey respondents believe the risk has increased."[45] We compound this misconception by factoring fear into everyday decisions—for example, choosing to drive rather than fly, due to the possibility of a terror attack. But doing so actually increases risk, because flying is statistically much safer than driving.[46]

Steven Pinker, Harvard psychologist, studied this topic in depth, and has shown that past decades had much more violence than the present. During World War II, three hundred of every one hundred thousand people each year were lost to war. During the Korean War it was twenty people per one hundred thousand. It then dropped to the teens during the Vietnam War and then fell to the single digits per one hundred thousand people. In the twentyfirst century it's been below one war death per one hundred thousand people per year.[47]

This is not to imply that any level of violence is acceptable, but the world is making progress, despite all the news coverage. Violence has actually decreased and is less pervasive than at any time in history. The reason? According to Pinker, it's because we are getting smarter.

Pinker's studies of IQ tests show the average teenager is smarter with each generation. IQ test scores are adjusted over time, so 100 remains average. But if you were to keep the test the same, a teenager who scores 100 today would have scored 118 in 1950 and 130 in 1910. This year's average kid would have been a near genius in 1910, and generally, with increased intelligence comes an increased adversity to violence. We find more advanced ways to "turn swords into plowshares."[48] And we need to use these smarts for more than turning away from violence. We need to fight this human desire for stories, especially gruesome ones, and our media's incessant coverage of negative events. How often have we seen good news headlines?

Likely, rarely. We need to understand that news covers what happened. It doesn't cover what didn't happen. That we have fewer violent crimes seldom makes the news, and the number of tragic stories far outweighs "good" news.

We also need to recognize that we are hearing and seeing more news than ever before. Events happening all over our world are brought to our attention daily. Twenty-four-hour news coverage is available in the palm of our hand. We need to avoid the barrage of negativity and maybe even decrease time spent watching or reading the news. Once a day is plenty.

A third strategy is more introspective. We need to pay attention to the ideas forming in our minds and question them. In the words of Euripides over 2,400 years ago, "Man's most valuable trait is a judicious sense of what not to believe." Seeking the truth through statistics is more important than ever. Let's not get caught up in the stories. In a nutshell, *we need to learn to live statistically*.

RR PO

1. *Your Money and Your Brain: How the New Science of Neuroeconomics Can Help Make You Rich* by Jason Zweig

2. *Don't Believe Everything You Think: The 6 Basic Mistakes We Make In Thinking* by Thomas E. Kida

3. *Predictably Irrational: The Hidden Forces That Shape Our Decisions* by Dan Ariely

4. *Sway: The Irresistible Pull of Irrational Behavior* by Ori Brafman and

R om Brafman

PART TWO

HOW OUR BRAIN CHANGES

*"*O*bserve constantly that all things take place by change, and accustom thyself to consider that the nature of the Universe loves nothing so much*

as to change the things which are, and to make new things like them."

—Marcus Aurelius

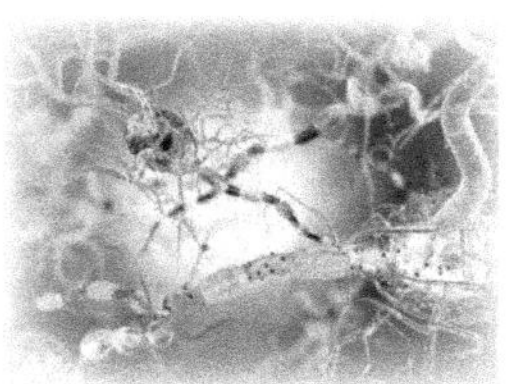

19. N

Neuroplasticity *is a big word driving big excitement. It refers to the brain's ability to change its own structure in ways before thought impossible.*

Atrue-life example will help.

For a few dark moments, imagine your three-year-old granddaughter was in a tragic accident. You're told by physicians that your granddaughter—we'll call her Lorie—has sustained severe brain damage and they're even recommending transferring her to a facility where she can pass in peace.

The damage is extensive. Many of the connections between the two hemispheres of Lorie's brain were either severed or severely damaged. But you notice something the doctors do not. When you look into her eyes, she seems to smile.

This really happened. Grandparents Cal and Janet (names changed) faced this frightful dilemma.

They did not give up. The smiles were the way they communicated with Lorie for months.

Janet wheeled Lorie down the hospital hall and Cal played games with her by hiding behind doors and jumping out yelling, "Boo!"—to which Lorie smiled. Yet the doctors still insisted nothing was there.

Fast forward eight years.

I first met Lorie when her grandfather brought her to a birthday party. She was beaming, chatty, articulate, and exuding an energy level only possible for an eleven-year-old. In every way, she seemed a normal energetic preadolescent, but more mature, as with the ease with which she chatted with her elders. Lorie brought an aura of sunshine and pleasantness to the room that everyone enjoyed. Her grandfather, Cal, was clearly proud of her.

Cal and Janet had not given up. Through the years they dedicated countless hours and persevered with various therapies and learning exercises based on concepts in succeeding chapters.

To prepare for writing this book, I met with Lorie's grandfather for an update. At this writing Lorie is a sophomore in high school and an athlete. She has swimming trophies and is competing with success at state levels. To look at her you would think *Olympian*. She has a ready wit, ribs her grandfather incessantly, and exudes excitement and sunshine.

Lorie's doctors at a prestigious hospital admit they have never been so happy to have been so wrong. She visits them annually, and tests show Lorie has grown many new connections between the two halves of her brain.

Per grandfather Cal, one of Lorie's favorite pastimes is riding in the family convertible (hoping soon to drive it) and playing Neil Diamond with the sound way up to "teenager" level.

One of her favorite songs is Neal Diamond's "Hell Yeah." If Lorie's story fascinates you, envision her riding off in the convertible singing at the top of her lungs with fist pumps in the air. Then look up the song lyrics. You'll gain a new appreciation for the song.

Growing new brain cells is not entirely unexpected of a young child. But at three years old, Lorie's brain was about 80 percent the size it would be as an adult. Could the final growth—20 percent—of Lorie's brain "fit in" to assist?

Lorie's brain was so severely damaged doctors found it difficult to believe. And, back then, scientists believed that current brain cells didn't reproduce.

But Lorie's brain defied all these prior concepts. Lorie's brain pulled off the miracle that is the stuff of neuroplasticity.

So how could her doctors have been so wrong?

Until the end of the twentieth-century, prevailing theories held that, though young children generated new brain cells, the adult human brain was hardwired after early formative years. In other words, upon reaching adulthood, we would develop all the brain cells we would get, and those cells were genetically coded to do certain tasks.

Scientists also knew connections (synapses) between brain cells (neurons) could change and that learning resulted from changing these connections (sprouting dendrites) or strengthening them. The accepted theory of "cells that fire together wire together," drove these concepts. In other words, the neurons that fired together in a chain changed in such a way that made it more likely that firing one would fire the other. Thus, "wired together."

And this was the extent of what scientists thought the brain could do. Now we know differently. Lorie's "neuroplasticity" was well beyond this retail variety of synaptic connection or strengthening. We're talking about wholesale changes previously deemed impossible. The brain is capable of reorganizing itself. The next several chapters discuss these miraculous changes.

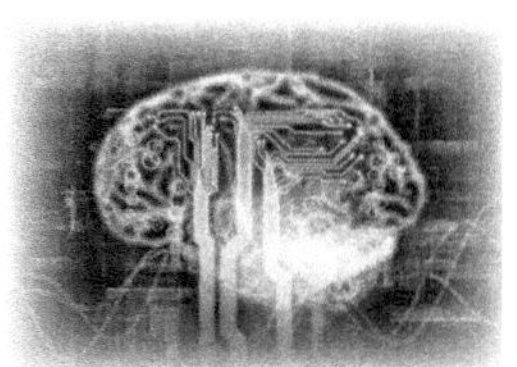

20. TR CE

*O*ur brain is capable of recruiting additional cortex for important tasks, cortex beyond those areas originally dedicated to certain functions. oted neuroscientist Alvaro Pascual-Leone of the Harvard Medical School conducted a deceptively simple experiment. He instructed volunteers to learn a five-finger piano exercise and try to play it as fluidly as possible while keeping up to a metronome's constant sixty beats per minute. They were asked to practice two hours a day, every day, for five days. Then it was test time.

N

Only this was not the proficiency test to which Harvard medical students were accustomed. Over the course of the five days, subjects underwent "transcranial-magnetic-stimulation" (TMS) testing to infer functions of neurons in specific locations in the brain. Scientists tested every day after practice to map how much of each volunteer's cortex controlled finger movements.

The part of the cortex dedicated to these finger movements expanded and "took over" surrounding areas of the brain "like dandelions on a suburban lawn," a result well beyond just strengthening connections.[49] The brains of these students were recruiting new neurons for the musical task at hand, neurons presumably previously dedicated to other, less-often-used functions. Other studies have confirmed the results—providing proof that greater use of muscles causes more cortex tissue to be devoted to that specific task.

This expansion of recruited cortex was contrary to prior genetic coded disposition theory. But it wasn't difficult to imagine, nor was it especially surprising.

But the next step was.

Pascual-Leone and his team continued the study but added a group that merely *thought* about the piano exercise. They imagined their fingers playing the piano part while keeping their hands still. Results were unexpected, to say the least: Volunteers who *only mentally practiced* recorded similar physical reorganization of their cortex.

Let's restate that.

Volunteers who did *zero* physical rehearsing, and only mentally imagined the practice, had physical reorganization of their cortex similar to participants who practiced physically!

This concept is used extensively today by athletes, musicians, and even people giving speeches. When you can't practice physically, a mental rehearsal can still be of great benefit.

Think of the possibilities. The following chapters explore in more depth.

21. C R

*O*ur brain is capable of recruiting additional cortex to replace cortex damaged from stroke or other injury.

T

He last chapter demonstrated the brain could expand areas designed to handle certain motor functions. But if a limb is severed or suffers nerve damage, what happens to that part of the brain?

Likewise, what happens if part of the brain itself is damaged, as in Lorie's case? Could the brain recruit other areas of the brain to replace damaged tissue?

The old dogma said, "absolutely not." Such thinking lowered therapy expectations for stroke victims and the prospects of fixing pathological wiring responsible for psychiatric disorders.

Scientists believed that certain clusters of neurons would process signals from your nose and other clusters of neurons would process signals from your fingers, and they'd do nothing else until the day you died. If you severed the nerve in your finger, the associated brain cluster should have "gone dark."

Michael Merzenich, PhD, and professor emeritus at the University of California at San Francisco, questioned these theories. In well-intended but controversial research, he severed the finger nerves of laboratory monkeys. Several months afterward, he found the part of the cortex that originally responded to the finger was now responding to signals from other parts of the hand![50]

Likewise, Edward Taub, PhD and behavioral neuroscientist at the University of Alabama at Birmingham, searched for solutions for stroke victims. He wondered if sensory feedback was necessary to move a limb. To find out, he surgically removed the sensory nerve from one or both arms of lab monkeys to stop all sensation from their limb(s). But before the experiment was finished, animal rights activists rescued the monkeys and removed them from the experiment.

However, twelve years later, scientists revisited the project. Several of the monkeys were to be euthanized to spare them further suffering. Aware of the original purpose of the experiment, the scientists persuaded authorities to allow a final examination of the monkeys' brains to determine what happened to the "arm" region of the brain after having no sensation for years.

It wasn't silent. It had changed jobs. It now processed signals from the face instead. And the region now responsible for receiving sensations from the face had grown 10 to 14 square millimeters, in what scientists described as "a massive cortical reorganization."[51]

The same phenomenon has been detected in humans. People blind from birth who become proficient in Braille provide evidence that the visual cortex can switch jobs to process tactile signals from the fingers.

But what about later in life?

Pascual-Leone took the next step. He blindfolded sighted volunteers for five days and had them spend their time learning Braille and sharpening their hearing. Brain scans were conducted before and after, with results confirming theory. When volunteers touched an object or heard sounds, activity in their visual cortex increased—a finding considered impossible by previous thought.[52]

So what could this mean for stroke victims?

Taub had inferred that, if stroke had damaged one area, the brain could recruit another to do the job. But if the brain could do this, why were stroke patients unable to use their affected limbs?

Taub reasoned that, in part, it was because of *learned non-use*: the patients stopped trying to use the affected limb. They had grown used to their disabled limbs and they assumed they could not make improvements.

If this was true, the trick was to *force* patients to use the affected limb. To do so, Taub put the "good" arm of his patients in a sling, forcing stroke sufferers to use their affected arm. And force them he did, with a whole regimen of exercises performed for 90 percent of waking hours over ten straight days. After this short but intensive rehab period, Taub found patients regained significant use of an arm they thought would dangle uselessly for the rest of their life.[53]

Taub's treatment was called constraint-induced therapy (CIT) and a larger later experiment found it superior to normal stroke therapy. Consequently, Taub has been hailed by the American Stroke Association as "at the forefront of a revolution." But, due to the intensity of the regimen and the intensive hours required of therapists, CIT has not been widely adopted, especially in the United States, where insurance is not likely to cover the extensive therapy.

Though the insurance companies are slow, the evidence is clear. Our brain can reorganize itself. Just ask Lorie.

So if you or a loved one experiences some type of brain trauma, be sure to press medical personnel for all the options and therapies. Perseverance pays.

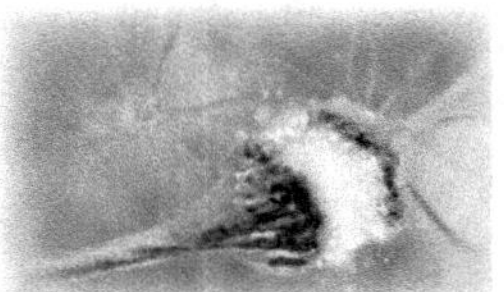

22. N

Despite even recent thoughts to the contrary, we can generate new brain cells, but not in the way we expected.

o what about these new brain cells? Do we really have all we are going to get by the time we're an adult? And if they aren't static, how does memory stay in place? How do we remember how to ride a bicycle if new cells are "tagged in" like wrestlers in a wrestling match?

S

Scientists knew neurons didn't divide, so they concluded new brain cell development was impossible.

And there were other reasons.

Considering the complexity of the brain, they couldn't imagine how new brain cells would assimilate. Expecting them to contribute "made as much sense as expecting a box of wires to improve an already running supercomputer."[54]

But what about Lorie? Did Lorie make new brain cells? And do older adults?

Animal studies were the first indications. In 1997 Fred Gage, Adler Professor in the Laboratory of Genetics at the Salk institute, conducted an experiment with lab mice using an enriched environment with steps, tunnels, wheels, toys, and lots of other mice. Other mice were placed in standard cages.

Compared to the standard cages, the enriched environment triggered the development of new neurons to the tune of 15 percent (from 270,000 neurons in the hippocampus to 317,000). It didn't matter how old the mice were. Senior citizen mice experienced even bigger boosts than the younger ones. The enriched environment, or something in it, was triggering the development of new brain cells, a process called "neurogenesis."[55]

At that time, neurogenesis was based only on animal studies, and wouldn't necessarily mean it would happen in humans. Human experimentation had significant roadblocks. For one, no form of non-invasive brain imaging existed to detect new neurons. And, animal studies involved euthanization to remove part of the brain for study under a microscope. Not an option for people.

Or was it?

Swedish neurologist Peter Eriksson, spending a sabbatical at Gage's lab, realized an opportunity may be available. Cancer patients were often injected with BrdU, a substance used to detect the spread of malignant cells. But BrdU would detect not only new cancer cells but also *any* new cell.

The light bulb went on. If BrdU could detect not only new cancer cells but any new cell, could it detect new neurons?

Eriksson sought permission from terminally ill patients and their families and physicians to do brain autopsies after patients had passed. Under the microscope he found BRdU tagged cells in the same location as neurogenesis was mapped in the animal studies. Patients had not received injections of BrdU until they contracted the disease, so cells marked by BrdU had to be generated after the injections.

Here was proof, contrary to prior dogma, that the adult human brain does generate new brain cells.[56]

Scientists were correct that brain cells do not divide, but new brain cells do come from another source. Our brains have a reserve called "neural stem cells," precursor cells capable of growing and differentiating into neurons and other types of nerve cells.[57]

So what causes neural stem cells to grow and differentiate into neurons and other cells? Back to the animal studies.

In a variation of the enriched environment experiment, Gage housed one group of mice in standard empty cages. Another group lived in cages with a running wheel they could use whenever they wished. (If you've ever had pet mice, you know the wheel would turn constantly all night!) The running mice produced twice as many new brain cells as the sedentary mice, suggesting physical activity alone generates new brain cells. After tweaking various environments Gage summarized his findings:

We think voluntary exercise increases the number of neural stem cells that divide and give rise to new neurons in the hippocampus. But we think it is environmental enrichment that supports these cells. Usually 50% of the new cells reaching the dentate gyrus of the hippocampus die. But if the animal lives in an enriched environment, many fewer of the new cells die. Environmental enrichment doesn't seem to affect cell proliferation and the generation of new neurons, but it can affect the rate and the number of cells that survive and integrate into the circuitry. [58]

Gage continued such experiments and concluded running mice were also smarter.

But there was another variable of interest: the "voluntary" aspect. Gage conducted another experiment allowing one group of mice to get on and off the exercise wheel whenever they wanted. Another group was forced to stay on a mechanized treadmill or get thrown off like a rag doll. The conscripted

mice did not display increased neurogenesis.[59]

So what does this mean for those couch potato friends of yours?

Well, dragging them involuntarily to the gym may be fruitless for brain capacity, but the exercise could still help in other ways. So maybe don't tell them about this experiment?

Following Gage's work, Brian Christie, of the University of British Columbia, zeroed in on the physical underpinnings of neurogenesis in the wheel-running mice. He found they also had more dendrites (the bushy little projections that receive signals from other neurons) and more spines on the end of the dendrites, thereby increasing sites by which they can receive signals from other neurons. In generalizing to humans, Christie surmised, "Exercise induced changes in brain structure [are] . . . viable [ways] to combat deleterious effects of aging." This may well be why an active life benefits brain function.[60]

In fact, Lorie went through extensive physical exercise and mental stimulation throughout her rehabilitation. As an extra reward, she became an athlete.

So exercise is key. We don't have to become an athlete but we do need to keep moving to keep those new brain cells.

More on this and related concepts in later chapters.

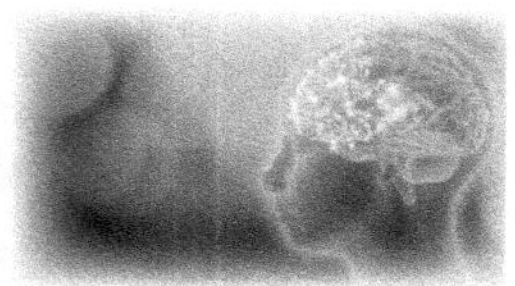

23. T C

*T*houghts can physically change the brain in beneficial ways.

So far we've seen the brain is much more malleable than before thought, and changeable through life experiences, at least of the physical kind.

But what about thoughts?

Remember Pascual-Leone's piano experiment, in which the brain recruited more cells based on just mental practice. Could the brain reorganize based on just thoughts? How do we tell? And how do we measure thoughts?

We know master musicians have increased brain real estate devoted to their skill. But what about masters of pure mental prowess? Or thought control? Comparing the masters with novices would help detect differences in brain patterns associated with thought control.

Malcolm Gladwell, in his book *Outliers*, found it takes ten thousand hours of practice to achieve mastery in a field. But who would have ten thousand hours of practice at thought control?

Monks. Monks who spend thousands of hours meditating.

Richard Davidson, PhD and noted neuroscientist at the University of Wisconsin, met with the Dalai Lama to discuss the science of the mind, and implications from the Buddhist perspective. The Dalai Lama was intrigued. He concluded that Buddhist concepts of mental transformation could be parallel with the plasticity of the brain.[61]

With the help of the Dalai Lama, Davidson recruited Buddhist monks to travel to Madison, WI, and meditate under his fMRI brain scan tube while he measured their brain activity. As a control he recruited students who had only a crash course in basic meditation techniques.

The monks showed significantly greater activity in the brain network associated with empathy than the novices.

But the most striking difference was the activity in the left prefrontal cortex, the site that marks happiness (more on this later). In the monks' brains, the left prefrontal cortex far exceeded activity of the right prefrontal cortex, the area associated with negative moods. By comparison, the control group showed no such difference. This was firm evidence that the "masters" could develop a change in neural patterns associated with happiness.

Accordingly, Davidson suggests this positive state is a trainable skill .[62] A trainable skill.

We can train ourselves to be happier. And we don't have to meditate for ten thousand hours. See chapters 35 through 37 for more on the science of happiness.

The following chapters will provide additional insight.

24. D N

L

We can take action to direct our brain to change in desirable ways. et's think about Davidson's comment about happiness as a trainable skill. That's powerful. Are other mental states trainable as well?

Let's look at examples.

Jeffrey Schwartz at UCLA experimented with mindfulness based cognitive behavior therapy (MBCT) to see if it could quiet the circuits underlying obsessive compulsive disorder (OCD) behavior. He taught patients a type of mindfulness therapy based on Buddhist meditation, emphasizing paying attention to one's thoughts. He then conducted before and after brain scans to see if meditation had an effect. Activity in the part of the brain known for the OCD circuit dropped dramatically, and, in exactly the same manner as patients using prescribed drugs. Schwartz called it "self-directed neuroplasti city."[63]

Scientists at the University of Toronto conducted similar experiments by teaching depressed patients to view their thoughts differently. Fourteen patients underwent MBCT while thirteen others received Paxil, a standard antidepressant drug. They expected effects to be similar, and they were. All participants improved comparably after the experiment.

But the big surprise was the brain scans.

MBCT muted activity in the frontal cortex, the area where unwanted ruminations are seated. Paxil *raised* activity in the same place. MBCT increased activity in the "hippocampus of the limbic system" or the center of the brain's emotions. Paxil lowered activity here.

Toronto's Helen Mayberg explains, "Cognitive therapy targets the cortex, the thinking brain, reshaping how you process information and changing your thinking pattern. It decreases rumination and trains the brain to adopt different thinking circuits."[64] Later studies confirmed the improvements experienced by the MBCT patients were still present after two years. The patients on drugs needed to stay on them to maintain positive changes.

(Note these two studies were rooted in mindfulness-based *meditation*. Meditation is being taught in medical schools and in over two hundred fifty hospitals. It has been adopted by high-profile, success-ful people including Phil Jackson, Arnold Schwarzenegger, Rick Rubin, Tony Robbins, Ellen DeGeneres, Michael Jordan, Arianna Huffington, Rep Tim Ryan D-Ohio and many more. In fact, according to the National Center for Complementary and Integrated Health, about eighteen million adult U.S. citizens were practicing meditation in 2012. Many more are doing so now. If you are interested in more information on meditation, check out Appendix I.)

Educators are also experimenting. Seventh graders taught principles of neuroplasticity performed better on achievement tests than their peers.[65] Just knowing that your brain can change can be empowering.[66] Students found the revelations liberating and believed they could get smarter through study and practice.

Norman Doidge, author of *The Brain That Changes Itself,* says, "Everything to do with human training and education has to be re-examined in light of neuroplasticity."[67]

Richard Davidson pioneered another more direct experiment. He developed a "Kindness Curriculum" (KC) for preschoolers and kindergarteners that included age-appropriate mindfulness and lovingkindness meditation.

Children were given stickers and two envelopes: one for themselves and one with a picture of a sick child. They were told they could keep as many stickers as they wanted or they could also give some to the sick child. Over the course of the year, children in the KC group maintained initial levels of giving, while the control group became more selfish.[68]

In addition, compared to controls, the KC group developed significant gains in self-control, as measured by delayed gratification. Based on reports from teachers, they also ranked higher in learning, health, and social/emotional capacity compared to their peers. But more significantly, they also displayed more pro-social behavior and altruism. In summary, much can be done to direct our brain to rewire itself. Davidson's book, *The Emotional Life of Your Brain*, is an excellent source for methods to induce directed neuroplasticity. He explains development of emotional styles as well as the acquired skill of happiness. It's a highly recommended read. Davidson details specific meditation training to build attention, mindfulness-based training to deal with stress, and many other routines to build desired traits.

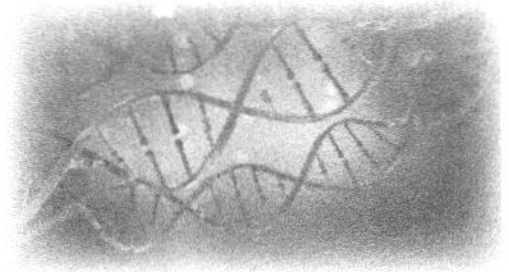

25. E

Thoughts can change the way we express our genes.

W

E just found that thoughts can physically change our minds in subs ways. But what about our initial foundation, our genetics? To what extent do our genes limit what we think and do?

Most of us would answer "a lot." We typically believe we were born with a set of genes that controls our lives, and we sense we are either victims or beneficiaries of those genes.

Evolutionary science supports these beliefs, implying much of human behavior is rooted in our evolutionary past. The science believes everything has an evolved purpose and explanation, which routes us right back to genetics, the code for how everything should unfold.

To be sure, our genes are significant. But how significant?

Brian Dias and Kerry Russel conducted a famous experiment at Emory University. They made mice afraid of one, and only one, fruity odor by pairing the odor with a mild shock. The fear-conditioned mice understandably developed more nose neurons sensitive to the smell. Then ten days after the fear conditioning, Dias and Russel allowed the mice to mate.

Here's the surprise: *Their offspring showed an increased startle to the fruity smell even though they had never been exposed to it.* And, they weren't fearful toward other smells.

Researchers then allowed the second generation of mice to mate and the same behavior surfaced in the third generation. The experiment was then repeated using *in vitro* fertilization, in case the parent mice were somehow training the offspring, even though the offspring had no contact with the fruity smell. The in vitro group yielded the same result. It proved the expression of genes was modified.[69]

In these experiments, researchers examined the *offspring* of mice to prove that *genes* were being modified. But gene expression is ongoing *in our own bodies* as our cells repair and reproduce. So modified gene expression is not limited to offspring. It could happen in our own bodies.

The same scientists found at least one mechanism responsible for this change in expression: DNA methylization. A methyl group ($CH3$) is part of a larger organic molecule. Methylization occurs when methyl groups attach to millions of spots along the mouse genome and affects the expression of nearby genes.

The good news is we really don't need to understand the mechanics of methylization. We can treat it like a black box. We just need to know what goes in and what goes out. So the next question is what goes in to that black box or, in essence, what affects methylization?

The answer is straightforward. It boils down to the very human activities of aging, exercise, diet, smoking, environment, training, thoughts, and others. You can guess the good ones over the bad.[70]

This idea of gene expression being regulated by environment, training, thoughts, and other influences has triggered a new science called "epigenetics." And it's getting a lot of attention.

Bruce Lipton, PhD and former researcher at the Stanford University School of Medicine, takes issue with the hype surrounding the Human Genome Project. He thinks perceptions, thoughts, and beliefs have a bigger impact on people's health than their genes.[71]

Let's say that again. Perception, thoughts, and beliefs have a bigger impact on health than genes?

Lipton says genes continually adapt depending on the needs of cells in a changing environment. Even our perceptions can change the expression of our genes.

Lipton is not alone. Dr. Richard Davidson at the University of Wisconsin, one of the foremost researchers on the brain and emotions, describes genes as, "dynamic in their expression."[72] They can be turned up or down by our experience, environment, and training.

With the birth of epigenetics comes empowerment in shaping our brains. We don't have to be victims of our DNA.

Davidson says, "We have an extraordinary ability to transform our minds, if we so choose."[73] He continues, "We have far more control over our wellbeing, over how we respond to the world, than a simplistic deterministic view would permit."[74] The new science leaves us with a more optimistic message and even confers responsibility. It empowers us to take ownership of our own minds.

Taking more responsibility for our minds is not an entirely new idea. For years, Buddhists have viewed mental attributes—temperament, for example —as skills to be cultivated. The new science supports this perspective, telling us traits like resilience, attention, and social intuition are trainable. Davidson explores these issues in depth in *The Emotional Life of Your Brain* and the more recently published *Altered Traits,* by Goleman and Davidson. Refer to these books for more insight.

"To them that ask, 'Where have you seen the gods, or how do you know for certain there are gods, that you are so devout in their worship?' I

answer, 'Neither have I ever seen my own soul, and yet I respect and honor it.'"

–Marcus Aurelius

Wouldn't it be great if religion told us everything we need to know? Wouldn't it make life's decisions easier?

We do have religions making such claims. In the U.S. the extreme right evangelical Christians advance a political agenda of intolerance toward gays, immigrants, and, at times, Muslims. Likewise, Muslim extremist terrorists use horrible violence to inflict their religious beliefs on others. Unfortunately, this is not new in history. Consider the Crusades. We have reasons to believe that organized religions don't "get it right."

Most religions are exclusive, claiming to be the only true religion. If you don't believe in their doctrine, no eternal life for you! This is like saying God is only in one room and not others.

Then which religion is right? Who's wrong? How can we tell? Can we seek truth in the ancient scriptures that are the source of many of today's religions?

Seeking truth amid the underlying motives of the church means acknowledging time lapses between writings and events and realizing the likelihood of inaccuracies. Yet this doesn't mean there is no

God. It just means the human beings, relaying their thoughts and observations, gave it their best shot but were as human as any of us in their capacity for error. And, since we are discussing a topic that is, by definition, beyond comprehension, how can we expect religious leaders to absolutely "get it right?"

Yet their efforts are not without fruit. People gathered together as a church can draw from one another and do great things for humanity. Perhaps the wise soul needs to be alert for the false teachings of humans but still be ready to absorb the essence of spirituality and be open to new discoveries of science in making sense of spirituality.

Our own upbringing weighs heavily on our perspective. Personally, I was raised Christian and try to follow the essence of Christ's teachings. Yet, I am wary of misinterpretations and, like Thomas Jefferson, I believe parts of the Bible cannot be true. (See Jefferson discussion below). And I have a problem with Christianity's exclusivist claim of being the only true religion. As described above, that's like saying God is in one room and not the other. And I certainly have a problem with the intolerance of right-wing Christians.

But that doesn't mean that the religion itself doesn't have a vital offering, if taken by the essence. I think of Christianity as being just one facet and one glimpse of a beautiful, multifaceted diamond. Other religions may provide another facet, again, taken by the essence and not necessarily by the doctrine of their leaders. If we could see through all facets, perhaps we could see the real beauty of the diamond.

But to review all religions is way beyond this exploration. However, we can explore the essence of one. By essence, I mean a truth contributing to our understanding of our condition as humanity, like the moral of the story.

For me, the most appropriate path is to use Christianity, the religion I was taught from childhood. But I am confident these principles apply to other religions.

Jesus Christ is one of the most famous, impactful persons to live on this planet. The Christian religion is the most popular on the planet with over two billion followers. Islam is second with 1.6 billion. (Muslims also acknowledge Christ and his teachings but relegate him to a prophet status.) So Christianity has, indeed, affected many lives. It is a message is of love, forgiveness, and salvation of our souls because of Christ's sacrifice of himself on the cross.

Most Christians believe Christ was the son of God and, therefore, our link to God. However, disagreement about interpretations of the Bible have spawned many Christian denominations and churches through the ages. Though Jesus walked the earth until about 30 AD, the earliest recountings of his teachings, or the gospels of the Bible, were not likely written until about 70 AD, soon enough for eyewitness recountings, but a long time for accurate memory. Biblical scholars have plenty to debate and research, but they universally agree that Christ did live and had a powerful impact on his followers.

One of the most famous forefathers of the U.S., Thomas Jefferson, had intense interest in the Bible. He believed Christ's teachings to be, "the most sublime and benevolent code of morals which has ever been offered to man." But he also studied it so carefully that he came to believe Christ's followers, who we assume wrote the gospels of the bible, combined Christ's gems of wisdom with their own political agendas. He didn't feel it was difficult to tell the difference. He took a razor blade and cut out parts he felt to be true and reassembled a slimmer, purer recounting of Christ's teachings. The old Bible with razor blade cuts has been on display at the National Museum of American History in Washington, D.C.

So how do we make sense of all this second-guessing? Who's right?

Which interpretation is right? What is the truth?

When we ask such questions, we are implicitly asking for the most reliable guidance from the past or the empiricism of science. Though science is discovering the beauty of the universe, it is questionable that science can resolve issues of divinity that, by definition, are beyond our comprehension. Likewise, though science is assisting us in reconstructing history, it is doubtful that we'll ever be able to reconstruct exactly what happened two thousand years ago. And we have already seen how reliance on the past can keep us in a "world is flat" condition. Maybe it's more important to look within ourselves and our actions and results.

Christianity has been the basis for many alcoholics' recovery and has provided a source of great personal strength to many. We've all known people who have experienced healing or almost mystical experiences. Are these and many others truly the result of divine intervention or a benefit of the mind's orientation or religious training? Such thoughts will be eternally subject to question. But the benefit was there.

Christianity (as well as other religions) has also united people to accomplish great things. Check out the You Tube video "One Dallas 2016" or the movie *Woodlawn* for real-life examples of recent events.

Many people have found unification, peace, direction, and joy from Christ's teachings. Church missions have provided much aid to people in need. Many acts of kindness and love have been created. Human beings have the capacity to draw together for such acts of love.

As Jesus said, "God is Love." So people drawing together and creating acts of love are creating acts of divinity.

Jesus also said, "The Kingdom of God is within us." Perhaps that is literally true. Could not a detailed factual historical basis be *irrele-*

vant if the Kingdom of God is truly within us and followers can draw from each other to create acts of love? Perhaps our minds contain so much more capacity than we think.

Regarding the truth, perhaps one of the greatest essays is the editorial written by Francis Pharcellus Church in the September 21, 1897 edition of the New York *Sun*. It is history's most reprinted newspaper editorial. Church writes a reply to a little girl who asks if there is a Santa Claus. Here is the editorial:

DEAR EDITOR: I am 8 years old.

Some of my little friends say there is no Santa Claus. Papa says, 'If you see it in THE SUN it's so.'

Please tell me the truth; is there a Santa Claus?

VIRGINIA O'HANLON.

115 WEST NINETY-FIFTH STREET

VIRGINIA, your little friends are wrong. They have been affected by the skepticism of a skeptical age. They do not believe except what they see. They think that nothing can be which is not comprehensible by their little minds. All minds, Virginia, whether they be men's or children's, are little. In this great universe of ours man is a mere insect, an ant, in his intellect, as compared with the boundless world about him, as measured by the intelligence capable of grasping the whole of truth and knowledge.

Yes, VIRGINIA, there is a Santa Claus. He exists as certainly as love and generosity and devotion exist, and you know that they abound and give to your life its highest beauty and joy. Alas! how dreary would be the world if there were no Santa Claus. It would be as dreary as if there were no VIRGINIAS. There would be no childlike faith then, no poetry, no romance to make tolerable this existence. We should have no enjoyment, except in sense and sight. The eternal light with which childhood fills the world would be extinguished.

Not believe in Santa Claus! You might as well not believe in fairies! You might get your papa to hire men to watch in all the chimneys on Christmas Eve to catch Santa Claus, but even if they did not see Santa Claus coming down, what would that prove? Nobody sees Santa Claus, but that is no sign that there is no Santa Claus. The most real things in the world are those that neither children nor men can see. Did you ever see fairies dancing on the lawn? Of course not, but that's no proof that they are not there. Nobody can conceive or imagine all the wonders there are unseen and unseeable in the world.

You may tear apart the baby's rattle and see what makes the noise inside, but there is a veil covering the unseen world which not the strongest man, nor even the united strength of all the strongest men that ever lived, could tear apart. Only faith, fancy, poetry, love, romance, can push aside that curtain and view and picture the supernal beauty and glory beyond. Is it all real? Ah, VIRGINIA, in all this world there is nothing else real and abiding.

No Santa Claus! Thank God! He lives, and he lives forever. A thousand years from now, Virginia, nay, ten times ten thousand years from now, he will continue to make glad the heart of childhood.

Hmmm. "Nobody can conceive or imagine all the wonders . . ." and ". . . there is a veil covering the unseen world . . . only faith, fancy, poetry, love, romance, can push aside that curtain and view and picture the supernatural beauty and glory beyond."

Maybe it's not what really happened two thousand plus years ago, but what does happen in lives of people who believe that stories such as those in the Bible can carry a greater truth and lead us to discovering higher truths within ourselves. And, perhaps this is the essence of Christianity and other religions as well.

9 781805 109655